McCordsville Elementary
Media Center

ONATHAN LONDON • PAUL MORIN

WHAT
THE
ANIMALS
WERE
WAITING
FOR

Scholastic Press

New York

Library of Congress catalog card number: 2001-131864
ISBN 0-439-33630-9

10 9 8 7 6 5 4 3 2 1   02 03 04 05 06
Printed in Canada

The paintings in this book were created with mixed media
(grit, sticks, sawdust, acrylics, and alkyds) on canvas.
The artwork was photographed by Fred Hunsberger. Vignette photos by Paul Morin.
The display type was set in Acropolis Now.
The text type was set in 18 point Cantoria.

First American edition, April 2002

To the Maasai, who persevere
J. L.

To Palmer's grandmothers, Verna and Janette
P. M.

You are Maasai.
You stand on one leg, like a stork, in the sun.
You are hot and your stomach growls.
These are the Months of Hunger,
says Grandmother.

The cows and goats are hungry, too.
The sun has burnt the sea of grass.
In the distance, you see gazelles, waiting.

What are they waiting for, Grandmother?
Why are they waiting?

You shall see, Tepi. You shall see.

It is time now, time to go home
with the bony cows and goats. The striped horses
of Africa — the zebras — swish their tails and wait.

What are they waiting for, Grandmother?
Why are they waiting?

You shall see, Tepi. You shall see.

Next day, the sun finds you again on the high savanna.
Cowbells tinkle. And over there, a family of elephants
munches dry grass, flaps huge ears like slow fans, and waits.

What are they waiting for, Grandmother?
Why are they waiting?

You shall see, Tepi. You shall see.

In the Mara River,
hippos stay cool.
Crocodile eyes
rise, and watch, and sink.
Something
will come surging
across the river,
but not now. Now
is the time of waiting.

Nearby, a huge herd of wildebeest
stands still as stones.
Giraffes sway in the tall acacias.
Then they stop.
Their ears turn.

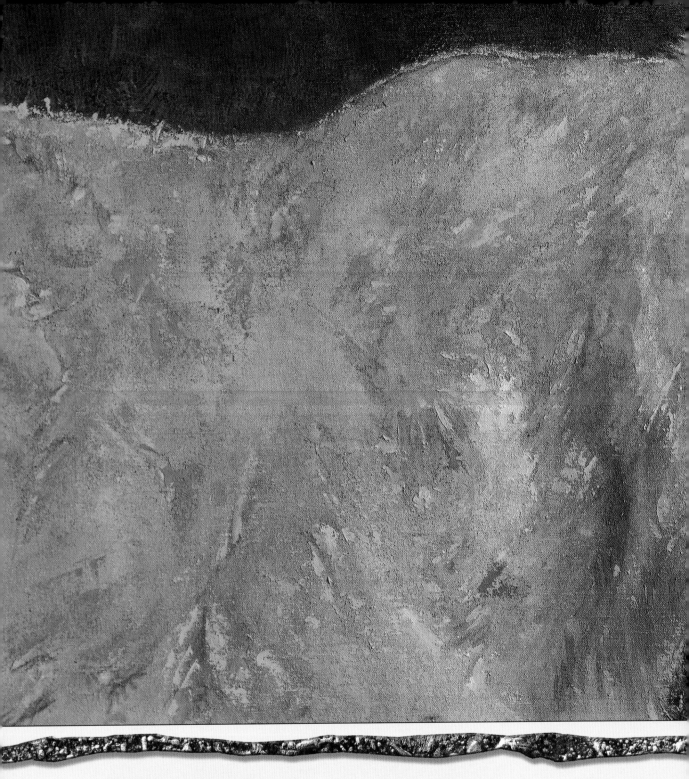

Simba! you cry.
Simba mbili! A big lion!
On a low rise, a mother lion gazes.
Her gold eyes shimmer with hidden lights.
Behind her, her mate watches and waits.

What are they waiting for, Grandmother?
Why are they waiting?

You shall see, Tepi. You shall see.

Afternoon comes, and a rumbling
ROOAAAARRRRR rolls across the plains.
Is that a lion, Grandmother? Or thunder?
The sun hides and the sky grows dark.

*Now, Tepi. Now you shall see
what the animals were waiting for.*

Suddenly, a wall of water comes crashing down.
Lightning scribbles. Thunder booms.
Rain, Grandmother! The rain is coming!

And something else. A deeper rumble.
The animals — they are stampeding,
racing toward the rain.

The giraffes lope. The wildebeest thunder
across the high plains, then plunge
into the Mara River and surge across.
Hippos grunt. Crocodiles lunge.
And the wildebeest scramble up the far bank
toward the promise of new grass.

Elephants move in a swaying mass.
Zebras gallop.
And the gazelles dance across the open plains —
bouncing, bouncing, bouncing.

You watch, and then you run.
You run home with the cows and goats.

And between rains, you get ready
as Grandmother waits with a friend
outside your hut.
They are dressed
for a special occasion.

And that night, as the edge of the moon
cuts into the sky,
you celebrate.
You sing and dance and feast.

And the elders tell stories
about the great migration,
which comes when the rains fall
and the great herds race
toward the first flush of new grass.

*New grass for our cows
and goats, too!* you sing.
*Now we can fill our gourds
with good fresh milk!*

Yes, Tepi, says Grandmother.
The Months of Hunger are over.

You are Maasai.
And now you know
what the animals were waiting for.

DATE DUE

Demco, Inc. 38-293